For Stella

First edition 2014

Library of Congress Catalog Card Number 2013943104

ISBN 978-0-7636-1495-9

13 14 15 16 17 18 TLF 10 9 8 7 6 5 4 3 2 1

Printed in Dongguan, Guangdong, China

This book was typeset in Triplex Serif.
The illustrations were done in watercolor, gouache, pastel,
ink, and colored pencil on sanded paper.

Candlewick Press
99 Dover Street
Somerville, Massachusetts 02144

visit us at www.candlewick.com

Stella's Starliner

ROSEMARY WELLS

CANDLEWICK PRESS

Stella lived in a house by the side of the road.
The house was completely silver.
It was as silver as a comet in the sky.
It was called the *Starliner*.

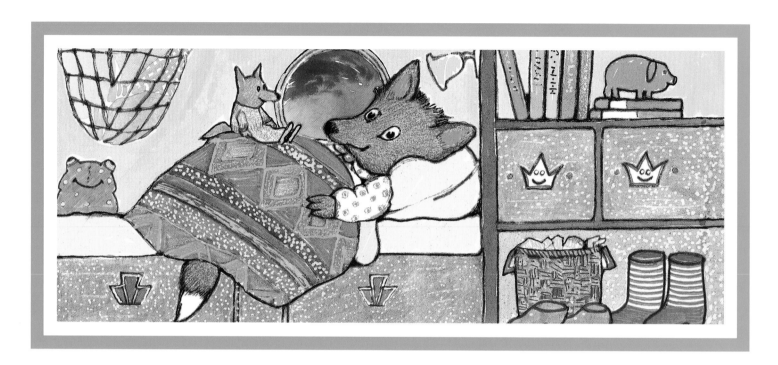

Inside was a room for sleeping and a room for being awake. There was a kitchen and a radio and a sofa that turned into a bed at the touch of a button.

Stella had everything she needed in her silver home.

Saturday night, Stella's daddy came home in his truck.
He parked it outside the Starliner.

Sunday morning, Stella's mama made pancakes for three
in the tiny kitchen.

Stella's daddy took Stella fishing on Sunday afternoon.

When the sun went down, Stella's daddy kissed Stella and her mama.
He gave them all the money in his pocket. Then he started up his truck
and went to work for another week. Stella and her mama waved him
all the way down to the end of the mountain road.

On Monday morning Stella and her mama went to market.
"We'll make peach cobbler," said Stella's mama.
"And corn chowder," said Stella.

Later, all the boys and girls cheered when the bookmobile came.
Stella and her mama read their books until they knew them
by heart. Stella didn't have a worry in the world.

Then one day a band of weasels passed by after school.

"Is this where you live?" the weasels asked Stella.

"Yes!" said Stella, "It's my silver home."

"Silver!" giggled one weasel. "Tin can is more like it!"

"It's an old trailer is what it is!" said another.

"You must be poor!" chimed a third.

The weasels made jokes and snapped their gum all the way down the mountain road. Their words stung Stella's heart like the stings of bees.

At suppertime Stella could not eat.
She wanted to tell her mama about the weasels
but didn't want her mama to feel the stings, too.

Evening fell on the Starliner. Stella could not sleep.
Outside, the pine trees whispered in the wind.
Stella thought she heard the weasels turning cartwheels
in the night.

Late in the night, Mama came to Stella's bedside.
"Something is wrong with my Stella," she said.
So Stella told her mama about the stinging words.

Stella's mama gave Stella a kiss and said,
"Look out the window!"
Hundreds of tiny lights spun by.
"Where are we?" Stella asked.
"Sailing through the Milky Way!" said her mama.

"Daddy has hitched our Starliner to his truck.

He's flying us far away through the night."

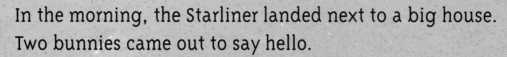

In the morning, the Starliner landed next to a big house.
Two bunnies came out to say hello.

One said, "I'm Grace and this is Stumpy."
"Is that your house?" asked Stumpy.
Stella didn't want to answer.

"Your house is made of silver," Stumpy went on.
"Sterling silver," added Grace. "You can tell."
"Our house is just plain old wood," said Stumpy.
"We want to see the inside!" said Grace.

Stella, Grace, and Stumpy played hide-and-seek in the Starliner's secret places. They turned the sofa into a bed and the bed back into a sofa with just the touch of a button.

"You must be a millionaire to live in a silver house," said Grace.
"A zillionaire," said Stumpy.

"A squillionaire!" agreed Stella.